Devil in the Drain

by Daniel Pinkwater

E. P. Dutton New York

Library of Congress Cataloging in Publication Data

Pinkwater, Daniel.
Devil in the drain.

Summary: A boy discovers the devil in a kitchen drain and fearlessly deals with him.
[1. Devil—Fiction] I. Title.
PZ7.P6335De 1984 [E] 83-16468
ISBN 0-525-44092-5

Published in the United States by E. P. Dutton, Inc.,
2 Park Avenue, New York, N.Y. 10016

Published simultaneously in Canada by
Fitzhenry & Whiteside Limited, Toronto

Editor: Ann Durell Designer: Claire Counihan

Printed in Hong Kong by South China Printing Co.
10 9 8 7 6 5 4 3 2 1 COBE First Edition

to the Hammocks

For a long time, I knew that the devil lived inside our plumbing. I could hear him making noises, especially down the drain of the kitchen sink.

Sometimes I would look into the drainpipe with a flashlight and try to see him.

Finally I caught a glimpse of something down there.

"Hey!" I said. "Are you the devil?"

"What if I am?" a voice from down the drain answered.

"I just want to know, that's all," I said.

"I don't have to tell you anything," the voice said.

"Come up here so I can see you," I said.

"Oh no! You'll turn on the water as soon as I get there, and get me all wet."

"No I won't, honestly."

"Well, that's what I would do."

"You *are* the devil, aren't you?"

"Yes."

"I'd really like to have a look at you. If I absolutely promise not to turn on the water, will you come up so I can see you?"

"Why do you want to see me?"

"I just do. Come on up. I won't hurt you. Besides, there are those little bar things across the drain. I couldn't get at you if I wanted to."

"I'm not afraid of you. I'm the devil."

"Then come up and let me see."

"All right—but if you turn on the water, I'll do some pretty bad things to you."

"You're really suspicious," I said.

"You would be too, if you were me," the devil said. His voice sounded closer.

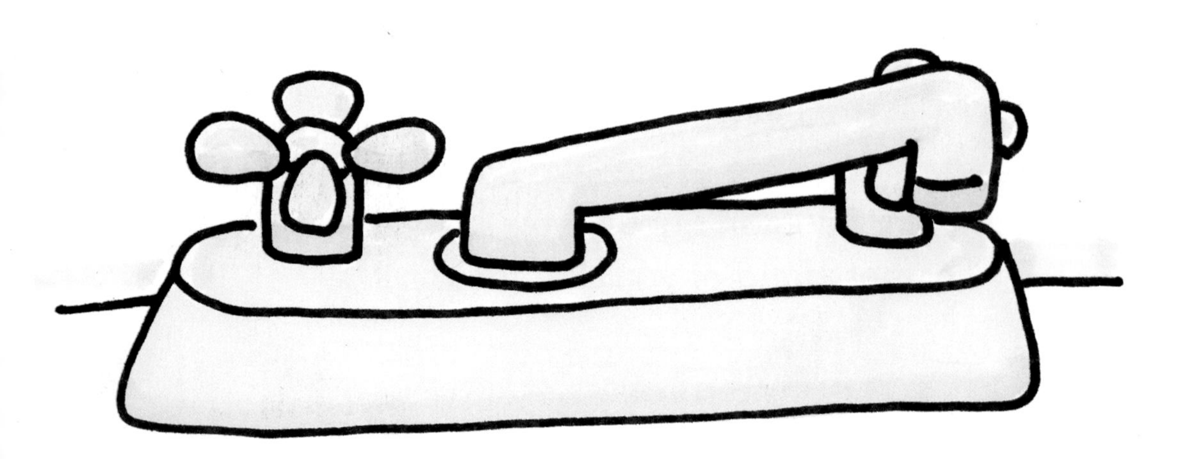

"Are you coming up?" I asked down the drain.

"Yes, yes, I'm coming," the devil said, "and don't say it's my fault if you get scared to death."

"I'm not scared," I said.

"Well you should be."

I could see the devil climbing up the drain. He was pretty small. He wasn't any bigger than the goldfish I had lost down that drain once, when I was changing the water in the fishbowl.

The devil got up to the little crossed bars. He had a face that reminded me of the fish, and he was almost the same color.

"Well, here I am," the devil said. "You're terrified, right?"

"Do you remember when I lost my fish down this drain?" I asked.

"Sure I do," the devil said. "You murdered him."

"I did not. It was an accident."

"Sure it was," the devil said. "Poor fish—he probably trusted you."

"The water overflowed, and he got sloshed out of the bowl and down the drain," I said. "I don't think he was smart enough to trust me or not trust me. Fish are dumb."

"That's right," the devil said, "tell yourself that. I heard him crying for help. You didn't even care."

"I did care," I said, "but I didn't kill him on purpose."

"But you admit you killed him."

"Is that what you do?" I asked.

"What?"

"Try to make people feel bad about things they can't help."

"It's one of the things I do," the devil said. "Now admit it—you feel pretty horrible about killing that fish, right?"

"I didn't kill him," I said, "and to tell the truth, I don't feel that bad about it. I'm sorry it happened, but it wasn't my fault."

"I'm getting bored talking about your stupid fish," the devil said. "How come you haven't mentioned how frightening I am, and at the same time sort of fascinating?"

"You look a little like a fish," I said. "How come you live in the plumbing?"

"Again with the fish!" the devil said. "I live in the plumbing because I can do whatever I please."

"How come you're so small?"

"I'm as big as I need to be," the devil said. "Now how about you getting me a pretzel? Do you have any of those skinny salty ones?"

I got the devil a pretzel. I pushed it down the drain. He ate it.

"That was lousy," he said. "I know you only got it for me because you're so frightened of me."

"Look," I said, "I got you the pretzel because you asked for it. You want another pretzel? I'll get you another pretzel. I happen to be a good-natured kid. And I am not in the least afraid of you."

"Yes I do," the devil said.
"Do what?"
"Yes I do want another pretzel."
"I'll get it."
"Ha! The kid's terrified," the devil said to himself.
I heard him say it. "That does it," I said.

I turned on both taps, hot and cold.
"Hey! No fair!" the devil shouted.

"Too bad," I said.

I heard the devil shouting and gurgling a long way down the drainpipe. He was really mad.

"That was a rotten trick!" he shouted. "You ought to be ashamed!"

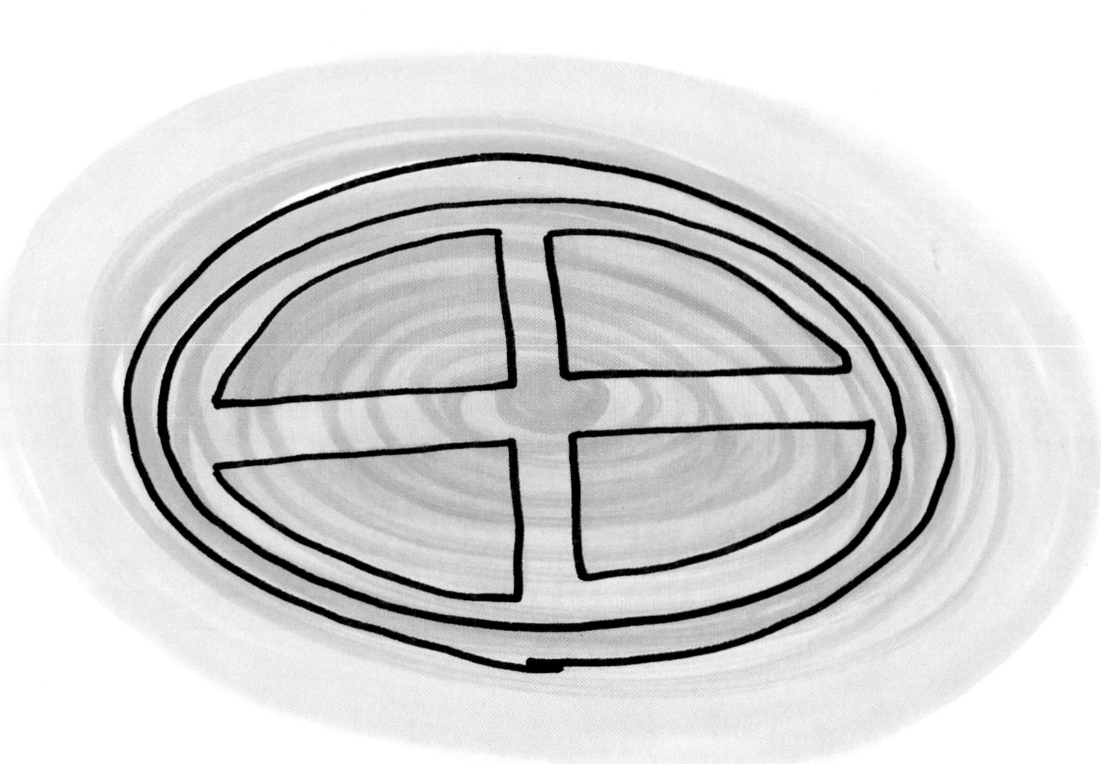